NOT TOO LITTLE TO KNOW

CHILDREN WHO WITNESSED THE ADVENT

KENNETH A WINTER

Illustrated by
CARLEY ELDER

WildernessLessons

Not Too Little To Know

Children who witnessed the Advent

Published by:

Kenneth A. Winter

WildernessLessons, LLC

Richmond, Virginia

United States of America

kenwinter.org

wildernesslessons.com

Illustrated by Carley Elder

Edited by Sheryl Martin Hash

Cover design by Dennis Waterman

ISBN 978-1-7341930-9-1 (hard cover)

ISBN 978-1-7349345-0-2 (soft cover)

ISBN 978-1-7349345-1-9 (e-book)

Library of Congress Control Number: 2020907096

CONTENTS

DEDICATION

To
Kordan and Kenton

But Jesus said, "Let the little children come to Me,
and do not forbid them; for of such is the kingdom of
heaven."
(Matthew 19:14 NKJ)

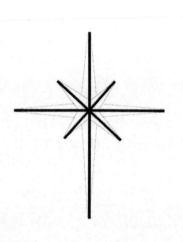

FROM THE AUTHOR

~

The stories in this book are a mixture of fiction and fact. They are fictional, first-person accounts from young men and women who witnessed events surrounding the birth of Jesus. At the end of each story is a brief explanation to help you understand what is true and what is imagination.

My hope is that these stories help you see the events surrounding Jesus's birth in a new way – and maybe through different eyes. Hopefully, you will see how Mary and Joseph's obedience to God came at a cost – one that followed them all of their lives. And they weren't the only ones. But they knew the cost was worth it!

Jesus's birth changed the lives of family, friends, neighbors, and even total strangers. Each young man and woman in this book also played a role in His story – just like you and i have the opportunity to play a role in God's story.

God is going to call on you to do things in your lifetime that require faith and obedience just like Mary and Joseph's. My prayer is that you will be like the young men and women in this book who know the truth and act on it.

The one common thread you will find in all these stories is Jesus. If you don't know Him already, my prayer is that you will come to believe in Him and know His love. Because the baby in the manger grew up to become the Man who died on the cross for our sins. But, that Man did not stay dead! He rose from the dead as our living Savior.[1] He is still very much alive and wants to have a personal relationship with you.[2] I pray that He is your Savior[3] – because no matter your age, you're **Not Too Little to Know**!

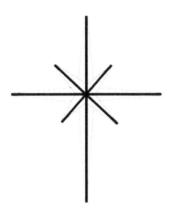

Isaac and his father as they see the ram caught in
the bushes

ISAAC'S STORY

*H*i there! My name is Isaac and I am the fourteen-year-old son of Abraham. A long time ago, God gave my father a promise. He told him, *"I will make you the father of a great nation. I will bless you and make your name famous, and you will be a blessing to many others. I will bless those who bless you and curse those who curse you; and the entire world will be blessed because of you."*[1]

When God gave my father that promise, my parents were already old and didn't have any children. My dad believed God would be true to His word, but he wondered how he could become the father of a great nation if he didn't have any kids.

My parents still did not have any children when my dad was eighty-six years old. My mom decided they couldn't wait any longer for God to give them a child. She told my father, *"Sleep with my servant, and if she has a baby, it will be mine."*[2] About nine months later, my mom's servant Hagar gave birth to a baby boy named Ishmael.

Instead of being happy about Ishmael's birth, my mom became jealous of Hagar. And my parents felt guilty because they had disobeyed God. Instead of trusting Him to provide the son He had promised, they had taken matters into their own hands. As precious as the life of little Ishmael was, he was not the son God had promised them.

Thirteen years later, God again came to my father and said, "By this time next year, your son Isaac will be born – and he will be the son of My promise."[3]

. . .

I was born when my father was one hundred years old. My parents were very happy. They praised God for keeping His promise. My father now understood he could trust God to always keep His promises. And that was a lesson my father taught me from an early age.

When I was a teenager, my love for God – and my father's – was put to the test. God told my father, *"Go get Isaac, your son, the one you dearly love! Take him to the land of Moriah, and I will show you a mountain where you must sacrifice him to Me on the fires of an altar."*[4]

So my dad and I, along with our two servants, got up early the next morning and headed to the mountains. We had been traveling for three days when my father told the servants to wait. He and I would go on alone for the rest of our trip. He laid the wood for the burnt offering on my shoulders, and he carried the knife and the flint to make the fire. As we climbed the mountain, I asked him, *"We have the wood and the flint to make the fire, but where is the lamb for the sacri-fice?"*[5]

I had never before seen the look on my dad's face as he tried to find the right words to say to me. He was trusting God for whatever happened next. So he said, *"God Himself will provide one, my son."*[6] I trusted him – and I trusted God – so I didn't ask any more questions.

The first thing we did when we arrived at the top of the mountain was build an altar. The altar was much like a table. We would use it to offer our sacrifice to God. The sacrifice would be our gift to God. My dad and I made the altar by setting a flat boulder on top of a pile of rocks we gathered. We laid out the wood for the fire on top of the boulder.

When it came time to put the sacrifice on the altar, my dad turned to me. I had watched him tie up the legs of lambs and goats many times when we were preparing a sacrifice. But this time, he began tying up my hands and feet. I didn't understand why, but I trusted him. I never struggled, even though I could have easily stopped him. After he finished tying me up, he laid me on top of the wood.

Tears were streaming down my father's cheeks as I looked up into his eyes. He raised a knife over his head like he was going to stab me. Suddenly, an angel of the Lord called out to him saying, *"Abraham, Abraham! Don't hurt the boy or do anything to him! Now I know that you honor and obey God, because you have not kept back your only son."*[7] Immediately, we saw a male sheep caught by the horns in some bushes nearby. I know that sheep wasn't there a moment before!

After my father removed the ropes from my hands and feet, we just stood there holding onto each other. We were so happy! After a while, we offered the sheep as a gift to God. An angel called out for a second time saying, *"Because you were willing to offer the Lord your only son, I will bless you and give you more descendants than stars in the sky or grains of sand along the beach. And through them you will be a blessing to all the nations on earth.*"(8)

My father had promised that God would provide a lamb – and He had! And one day, He would provide a lamb as a sacrifice for the world's sins. But when that day came, the lamb would be His Son.

My father and I had obeyed God that morning by climbing the mountain. Now as we walked back down, I knew that one day there would be another Father and Son who would climb that hill to offer a sacrifice. And I knew that Son would come as a baby in a very unusual way, and that He would somehow be a future member of my family.

I will tell my children one day how God kept His promise to my dad and they will tell their children who will pass it on to their children and grandchildren. And the promise of a coming Son will be told from family to family – until the day He comes.

∼

More about Isaac

Isaac is referred to as one of the "patriarchs" of the Israelites. A patriarch is one of the first fathers of a family that becomes a large group of people like the Israelites. When Isaac was an adult, he had two sons – Esau and Jacob. It was through Jacob that the promise of God continued. As a matter of fact, God changed his name from Jacob to Israel. It was through the future generations of Israel that Jesus came to be born as a baby.

You can read about the day Abraham and Isaac climbed to the top of the mountain in Genesis 22:1-19 in the Bible.

∼

Salome is a friend to Mary

SALOME'S STORY

$\mathcal{H}$ello! My name is Salome and I live in the town of Nazareth. It's not a very big town, so everybody knows everybody else. My family lives next door to Joseph the carpenter and his young wife, Mary. She is five years older than I am, and I have known her all of my life. When I was younger, she often helped my mother take care of me and I have always looked up to her like a big sister.

Eight months ago, Mary's father decided she would marry Joseph. He is a lot older than she is, but they seemed very happy. So, I was glad when Mary's father told the whole town that

Mary and Joseph would be getting married next year.

But four months later, their plans quickly changed. Joseph said they were getting married right then, and Mary went to live in his home as his wife. That night I heard my parents quietly talking about them. And I heard my mother say to my father, "Mary must be at least three months' pregnant. She has always been such a good girl. What has happened?"

The next morning, I heard some of our neighbors also talking about Mary and Joseph, saying they had done something wrong. "Mary is going to have a baby!" I thought. "What could be wrong about that? Why are people talking about her like she's done something bad?" Since Joseph was at work and Mary was home alone, I decided to go see her.

I could tell Mary had been crying. I walked up to her and gave her a hug. "Mary, I am so happy about your news!"

. . .

"What news have you heard, Salome?" Mary asked.

"That you are going to have a baby!"

"What else have you heard?" she asked.

"People are saying you and Joseph have done something bad," I said softly.

Mary looked sad as she told me, "My father, Joseph, and I told the rabbi and our other town leaders what has happened, but they don't believe us. They think we are making up the story and that we have done something wrong. But we haven't! We've told the truth – and it is news that everyone in town should be happy about."

"What news?" I asked.

. . .

"One day, soon after our engagement was announced, I was out taking a walk," Mary said. "Suddenly, an angel stood in front of me and said, *'Don't be afraid, Mary, because God is pleased with you. Listen! You will become pregnant. You will give birth to a Son, and you will name Him Jesus.'*[1] But I asked him, *'How can I have a baby? I am a virgin.'*[2] The angel told me, *'The Holy Spirit will come upon you, and the power of the Most High will cover you. The baby will be holy. He will be called the Son of God.'*[3]

"At the same time, the angel told me my cousin Elizabeth, who is very old, was also expecting a baby. So, I went to see her. When I got to her house, she knew right away that I was expecting a child and that He is the Son of God. Her child was chosen by God to tell the world about the Son I am carrying.

"After I returned home, that same angel came to Joseph in a dream and told him we were to go ahead with our marriage. The angel told Joseph that the child inside me is the answer to the

Scripture that says a pure woman will have a child who will save His people from their sins.

"But the angel did not tell us that many of our friends and neighbors wouldn't believe us."

"Well, I believe you, Mary," I said. "I know that you are telling the truth! I know you, and I know that you would not make up this story. You are special to God. Please don't be sad because of what others think and say. Be happy because of what God has given you!"

"Salome, my little friend," Mary said, "God brought you here to see me today. Just as He encouraged me through my cousin Elizabeth, He has encouraged me through you!"

When I got home, I told my parents about my talk with Mary. At first, they didn't know what to think. It sounded like something I made up. But, they also knew Mary and Joseph always told the truth. So, my parents believed them, too.

I started helping Mary with chores around her house whenever I had free time. Mary told me that my being with her cheered her up even more than the work I did. My mother told me that God placed me in Mary's life to be her friend when she needed a good friend.

A few weeks later, my parents told me we had to go to the city where my great-grandparents were born so we could be counted by our leaders. My family and I were headed to Hebron. Joseph and Mary would be going to Bethlehem. I was sad the day we all left home, but I knew God would give Mary another special friend to cheer her up along the way.

~

About Salome

Salome is not in the Bible. She was made up for this story. Mary would have been well liked in her village before the people learned that she was expecting a baby. Because she and Joseph had not yet finalized their marriage, there would have been neighbors who did not understand that her baby was the Son of God. Some of those neighbors would have treated Mary badly. But there were some, like Salome, who would have continued to be her friend.

You can read about the day the angel told Mary she would become pregnant with Jesus in Luke 1:26-38 in the Bible.

James travels to Bethlehem with his Uncle Joseph
and Aunt Mary

JAMES'S (THE SON OF CLOPAS) STORY

*H*i, I'm James and I am seven years old. I live in Cana, which is a town in Galilee. My father's name is Clopas, and his older brother is Joseph. My dad and my uncle Joseph are both carpenters. Years ago, my uncle moved to the nearby town of Nazareth to find work. My father stayed here to work with my grandpa.

I am learning how to be a carpenter just like my dad. He tells me stories about how he learned from my grandpa and my uncle. My uncle and my dad have always been close, even though my uncle is a lot older than my dad.

. . .

Uncle Joseph is with our family for most of our holidays, like this past spring when he went with our family to Jerusalem for Passover. Passover is an extra special festival for Jewish people because we thank God for freeing our people from slavery.

My mom and dad were afraid this might be a sad time for our family. My grandpa died last year, so this was our first Passover without him. But when we met up with my uncle he told us some happy news. He was engaged to be married to a young woman named Mary!

We had met Mary and her father when we visited Nazareth. We all liked her. And we were all really happy for Uncle Joseph. I did hear my parents say they were a little surprised by the news because Mary was a lot younger than my uncle. But my uncle's joy made us all very happy for him.

. . .

We had a great time together in Jerusalem and even saw my father's cousin Achim. A lot of his family was with him, including his grand-daughter Sarah. She is a little older than I am, but we had fun playing together – even if she is a girl! We were all happy that we would be to-gether again in December for Uncle Joseph and Mary's wedding in Nazareth.

My parents were surprised when my uncle and Mary came for a visit in May. After my mom – who is a really good cook – fed us lunch, all the adults went into another room to talk.

I could hear my uncle's voice as he began to talk.

"Soon after we got engaged," he said, "an angel came to Mary and told her that God had chosen her to have His Son. He is the One who God promised to Abraham and Isaac. He would be the Lamb who would be the sacrifice for the world's sins.

·   ·   ·

"The angel then told Mary to go visit her cousin Elizabeth, who was very old and didn't have any kids. But now Elizabeth was going to have a baby, too. And an angel told her that her son would one day announce the arrival of God's Son."

"Then," Uncle Joseph said, "the angel came to me in a dream and told me the same news. He also told me that Mary and I should get married now and not wait until December. So, that is what we have done.

"You are my family, so Mary and I wanted you to hear the news from us as soon as possible. We know all of this is a surprise, so please ask us any questions you have."

But my father didn't have any questions. He knew his brother was an honest man who did not lie. My uncle's word was all my father would ever need to hear to know that what he had just told my parents was true. So, my father looked at Uncle Joseph and Aunt Mary and said,

"We thank God for this news about His Son. We will pray for you as you get ready to be His parents.

"Mary, you are very special to God, and we are happy to have you join our family. And Joseph, my brother, you will be a great dad to this child."

Then they all started hugging each other so I walked into the room and joined them. Two days later, Uncle Joseph and Aunt Mary returned home to Nazareth.

My parents often talked about how our lives would now be different. My mom and dad were going to be aunt and uncle to God's Son, and I would be His cousin. I couldn't believe it! How could God send His Son to be a part of our family?

A few months later, my mom and dad said we had to go to Bethlehem so our family could be counted by our leaders. Uncle Joseph and Aunt Mary would be going, too.

My parents said we would all go together so we could help my aunt and uncle make the journey. When we got to Bethlehem, my aunt and uncle went to stay with our cousin Achim, while my parents and I went to stay with my mom's sister.

We arrived in Bethlehem knowing the baby would be born soon – but we didn't know how soon. God had chosen a special group of people to welcome His Son – but it wouldn't be our family – at least not that night!

~

About James (the son of Clopas)

There is a man by the name of Clopas in the Bible. [1] *He is a disciple of Jesus. Many people think that Clopas may have been Joseph's brother – more than likely a younger brother. There is also a man by the name of James, the son of Alphaeus.* [2] *Many people think that Alphaeus was another name for Clopas – and that James was the son of Clopas. This same James is sometimes referred to as James the Younger in the Bible.(3) He is one of the original twelve disciples of Jesus. So if this is true, the James in this story would have grown up to become not only a cousin of Jesus, but also one of Jesus's disciples.(4)*

You can read about Mary and Joseph's obedience to God in Matthew 1:18-25 in the Bible.

～

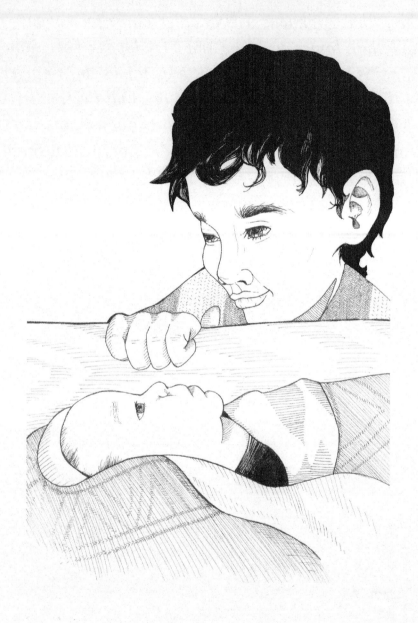

Shimon comes to the stable to see Jesus

SHIMON'S STORY

*H*i! Let me tell you a little bit about myself. My name is Shimon, and I am ten years old. My family has been watching over sheep in these Bethlehem hills since King David was a boy. I'm sure you have heard of him! He knew these hills like the back of his hand – just like I do.

I love helping my father take care of our sheep. My dad tells me God is the best Shepherd of all! He loves us and takes care of us. My father says when we take care of our sheep, we are being the most like God.

. . .

Most of the time, Bethlehem is a small, quiet town. But not long ago, our Roman emperor said we must go to the town where our ancestors were from so our leaders could count us. My dad was happy we already lived where we would be counted!

Our quiet town is now full of excitement. There are so many unfamiliar faces about town, and everyone is excited to see each other.

Last night, my dad, the other shepherds, and I were in the fields taking care of our sheep. It was a quiet night with no clouds in the sky. The sheep were resting and the town below us was still.

Suddenly, we saw a man with light shining around him. We had never seen anything like this before. We were all a little afraid so my father pulled me close to his side.

.   .   .

The man told us, *"Don't be afraid! I bring you good news of great joy for everyone! The Savior – yes, the Messiah, the Lord – has been born tonight in Bethlehem, the city of David! And this is how you will recognize Him: you will find a baby lying in a manger, wrapped snugly in strips of cloth!"*[1]

Then the sky was filled with many people who looked just like the man. We all fell to our knees in fear and covered our eyes from the bright light around them. We knew these were angels who had come to bring us great news. The angels began to praise God, saying:

"Glory to God in the highest heaven,

And peace on earth to those with whom He is pleased!"[2]

Time seemed to stop and nothing moved. Even the sheep seemed to bow down. Each one of us was overwhelmed by what we had just seen and heard.

.   .   .

Just as quickly as the angels appeared, they disappeared. We stood still, staring up into the sky. After a few minutes, we looked at each other and said, *"Come on, let's go into Bethlehem! Let's see this wonderful thing that has happened, which the Lord has told us about."*[(3)] I saw my father and the other shepherds do something they had never done before. They left our sheep without anyone to take care of them and protect them! We ran into town to the stable where the angels had told us to go.

As we approached the stable, we expected to find a lot of people gathered to see the newborn baby. We expected all of the religious leaders to be there – and perhaps even King Herod.

But no one else was there except the baby's mother and father plus a few animals. The baby was lying in the animals' feed box. Was this the right place? Was God's Son born in an animal stable? But we knew the answer was yes!

. . .

The baby's mother and father were kneeling on each side of the baby. They were surprised to see us, but they didn't tell us to leave. I looked at the baby's mother and she gently nodded her head that I could come closer.

We told the baby's parents about the angels and what they had said. The young mother smiled and seemed pleased to hear our news. Then we all fell to our knees and worshipped the baby lying before us.

We did not want the moment to end. We were all so happy we couldn't speak a word. The One who God had promised to Abraham and Isaac had now been born. And He was right there in front of us laying in a manger! We could not believe God had seen fit to tell a group of shepherds that His Son was born!

We could see that the baby's mother needed her rest. So one by one, we stood to our feet and began to quietly back out of the stable. I was the last one to stand up. As I looked at the baby, He seemed to be looking right back at me. It was like He could really see me, even though He had just been born! I kept looking at the baby until my father called for me to join him.

As we made our way back to the fields, we talked about all we had just seen and heard. We told people we saw about the baby and what the angel had told us. But no one seemed to care. I don't think they believed us. We went back to our sheep and they were right where we had left them!

This morning, I ran back to the stable to see the baby and His parents. But they were gone. I asked people near the stable about the baby, but no one seemed to know that a family had even been there, let alone who they were, or where they had gone. All that remained in the stable was the manger where the baby had laid, the animals that had surrounded Him, and my memory of that holy moment.

. . .

I didn't know the baby's name or where He had gone, but I did know who He was. He is the promised One – the Son of God!

~

About Shimon

Shimon is not in the Bible, but the shepherds are. The Bible tells us that the shepherds felt just like Shimon does in this story. Do you ever wonder what happened to the shepherds as they got older and Jesus became famous? Do you think they ran to see Him as an adult just like they did that night in the stable when He was a baby? i think they did! i even wrote a book about Shimon doing just that.

You can read about the shepherds in Luke 2:8-20 in the Bible.

~

Yanzu brings the gift of frankincense to Jesus

YANZU'S STORY

*H*i everyone! I am an eleven-year-old boy named Yanzu. I am not Jewish. I live in the city of Babylon which is in a very different part of the world. My city is the capital of what is known as the Parthian Empire. It is one of the best places for learning in the world, but I have not grown up hearing the stories about Abraham or Isaac – or the promised One.

I have a master whose name is Balthazar. When boys and girls from a poor family where I live turn ten years old, they must go to work. They become kitchen helpers, housekeepers, field workers, or people who work with their hands.

Some, like me, are fortunate enough to work for one of the important people of our city. My master's older brother is the governor, so my master lives in a palace.

Balthazar spends his days studying the stars. He sees things in the stars that others can't. He believes the stars help us know about important events that will happen. I am glad my master does not only see me as his helper, but also as one of his students. He is teaching me about the stars.

He has been studying a new star for the past year. He told me it is brighter than any he has ever seen. He says there are old writings by people called Israelites that tell of a King who will be greater than all the other kings. He believes this star is telling us about the birth of this great King.

A few weeks ago, my master told me we were going to follow the star to find this King. He said we would be taking a special gift to Him called frankincense, which comes from trees in our part of the world. It's used for many things – even to help heal sick people. My master trusted me to carry the chest that contained the frankincense and told me to make sure nothing happened to it. I was very happy and proud that he trusted me that much!

Before I went to sleep each night, I always looked up at the star in the sky. I would wonder what this King must be like. How powerful He must be! He must have more money and helpers than anyone else. Even as a baby, He would wear only the best clothes. He would live in a palace even better than the one my master lives in. I hoped I would see Him someday. But I feared that no one as lowly as me would ever be permitted to enter into His presence.

We had traveled for several days when we met another group of people. They were following the same star to find the King, too. These were wise men like my master, but they came from other countries. They invited my master to join them, and he said yes.

. . .

After a few more days of travel, it became clear that the star was leading us into Judaea – one of the provinces where the Israelites lived. My master and the other wise men decided to stop in the city of Jerusalem to visit the Israelite ruler, King Herod. My master believed King Herod would know where we would find the King we were seeking. As we entered the city, people stared and pointed at us. I couldn't imagine that they had never seen a caravan. But I could see they dressed very plainly. The bright colors of our clothing and robes must have looked very strange to them.

When we arrived at the palace, our masters were told they could enter to see the king but the rest of us would need to wait in the outer courtyard with our animals. My master in-structed me to stay with all of our belongings, including the chest of frankincense. The other servants were told by their masters to do the same. The palace servants were curious about the special gifts we had on the backs of our animals. They were surprised that our masters had not brought those gifts for their king.

After a long while, my master and the others returned to us and told us we would continue our journey. We would travel a little further to a small town called Bethlehem. King Herod had told my master that we would find the special King there.

Given the strange welcome we had received in Jerusalem, my master and the others decided not to ask anyone on the streets of Bethlehem to direct us. Instead they would trust the star to guide us. The star eventually stopped over a house that was built beside a hill. When my master and the other wise men knocked on the door, the master of the home greeted them. But like everyone else we had met along the way, he was very surprised to see us.

My master explained that they were there to honor the newborn King. "We have followed the star and it has led us to this home," my master said. A woman, who appeared to be the wife of the man at the door, stepped out from behind him and quietly told my master and the others to follow her.

The rest of us waited outside. I couldn't help but think this was a funny place for the special King to be staying. The house was very small and simple – not like a palace at all!

My master sent word for me to bring the chest into the house. The other wise men's helpers brought in their masters' gifts, too. We were led up to the third floor and down a narrow hallway to a small room. When I arrived at the door, my master motioned for me to enter the room. I was being allowed to enter into the King's presence!

As I walked into the room, I bowed my head and looked at the floor. I don't have the words to tell you how I felt. After I handed the chest to my master, I knelt down on my knees and kept my eyes lowered. I knew I was in the presence of One who deserved great honor.

My master kneeled, too, and gave his gift to the mother and baby. As he opened the chest, the sweet smell of frankincense filled the air. The smell caused me to look up. The baby's mother was smiling at us. She and the baby were dressed plainly – not in the fine clothing I had expected. But as I looked into His eyes, I knew He was the King!

I looked at my master as he too knelt before the baby. And I realized he and I were the same before this baby. This little One is the King before whom every knee must bow. I knew He was my King – just as much as He was my master's King. And I knew I would always be welcome in His presence.

I wanted to stay in the room with the baby forever! But soon my master said it was time for us to leave. "Yanzu," he said, "you have knelt before a special child tonight. He is not just any king, but the King of all kings. The star has led us to Him. Though we must leave Him now, be sure to keep Him in your heart wherever you go."

~

About Yanzu

Yanzu is not in the Bible, and neither is Balthazar by name. However, we do know that wise men traveled a long way to follow the star to a home in Bethlehem where Jesus was staying. The wise men and their helpers would have had many of Yanzu's same feelings when they met the baby Jesus.

You can read about the visit of the wise men in Matthew 2:1-12 in the Bible.

~

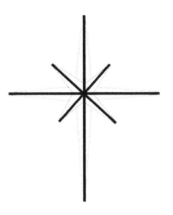

Sarah discovers her grandma with Mary and Jesus

SARAH'S STORY

*H*ello! My name is Sarah and I am eight years old. I live in the town of Bethlehem in my grandparents' home with my mom, dad, uncles, aunts, brothers, sister, and cousins. There are eighteen of us living in the same house. And my aunt is expecting a baby, so guess how many will be in our house then? Nineteen!

Our home is built into the side of a hill, and the stable where we keep our animals is a cave in the hill. Two years ago, my grandpa Achim added more rooms upstairs in our house. My grandpa says God has blessed him with a big family. He says if God gives us more kids, we'll just keep adding more rooms to our house! My grandpa, my dad, and my uncles are all carpenters, so that will be easy for them to do.

Not long ago, the Roman emperor said all the people in our land must travel to the town where their family was originally from in order to be counted. Our family is from this town, so we didn't have to go anywhere! But many of our cousins who live in other towns had to come here. And many of them were going to stay at our house.

Grandpa and grandma had all of us kids move into two rooms so our guests could sleep in our rooms. All of us helped my grandparents get ready for our cousins' visit.

My grandpa was really happy his cousin Joseph was coming. I was with my grandparents in Jerusalem for Passover earlier this year when they last saw him. My grandpa and Joseph acted like best friends. And grandpa saved a special room in the house just for him.

But then one night grandpa told us Joseph was not going to stay with us. We were all surprised! I saw grandma give my grandpa a strange look, but they didn't say anything.

Two days later I was walking through town and saw Shimon, the shepherd boy. He asked me about a baby born in our stable a couple of nights ago. I laughed because I thought he was being silly. But he said he wasn't playing – there really was a baby because he, his dad, and some other shepherds had come to see Him. And they had met the baby's parents, too.

Next he told me a wild story about angels and how they talked to the shepherds and told them to go see the baby. Then Shimon looked at me and asked, "Who were they?"

.   .   .

"I don't know," I said. "You're the one who saw them. Not me!" I decided Shimon really was making up a story!

Later that afternoon, I went to play with one of my cousins who lived in town. She had company staying with her family, too, including a little boy named James, his father, Clopas, and his mother. I had met James in Jerusalem. He had been with his uncle Joseph and his parents at Passover. James looked surprised when I told him our family was sorry that his uncle did not come to Bethlehem.

"Of course, he came to Bethlehem," James said. "He and Aunt Mary both came. Didn't you see them?"

"No," I told him. "They couldn't have come. My grandpa told us Joseph wouldn't be coming to stay with us."

. . .

"Well, they may not have stayed with you," James said, "but they came here. And Aunt Mary was going to have a baby."

"A baby!" I said with surprise. "Shimon told me he saw a baby in our stable."

"Who is Shimon?" James asked.

"He's just a shepherd boy I know," I told him. Then I left so I could get home and find out what was going on. I was really confused!

I told my grandma what Shimon and James had said. She was not surprised at all! She told me that my grandpa would not be happy if he heard me talking about this.

"I cannot tell you what has happened," Grandma said. "Grandpa will not let me. And you can't talk to anyone else about it. I hope one day I can tell you. But until then you must promise not to ask any more questions, and you must promise not to talk about it with anyone else, including your parents."

I promised my grandma that I would keep the secret. And I did!

One night we were eating supper and my aunt Tamar said she had heard a baby crying upstairs in the house. My grandma said, "With all the babies in this house, it's hard to tell where all of the cries are coming from! But each one is a joy."

Later that night, I saw my grandma go upstairs. She was carrying a small pot of food, so I decided to follow her. She went into the empty room that had been saved for Joseph. I quietly walked to the door. I could hear her whispering to someone. Then I heard soft, gentle sounds. "There's a baby in there!" I said under my breath.

.   .   .

My grandma turned her head to see me just as I stepped through the door. There was a young woman with her, holding a baby. At first my grandma looked angry, but then she smiled and told me to come in and close the door.

The baby had dark, curly hair and the most beautiful, brown eyes I had ever seen. I could not stop looking into His eyes. He smiled as if He knew who I was. He was not like any baby I had ever seen before. There was something very special about Him. The entire room felt peaceful.

"This is the baby the shepherd boy told me he saw in the stable, isn't He?" I asked.

"Yes, He is," my grandma said. "Sarah, this is Jesus. And this is His mother, Mary."

My grandma said that when Joseph and Mary came to our front door, she and my grandpa were surprised. They could tell that Mary was going to have a baby soon. Joseph told them how an angel had visited Mary and told her she was going to have the Son of God. That angel later told Joseph the same thing. So, Joseph married Mary even though she was already pregnant.

My grandpa didn't believe Joseph. He thought Mary and Joseph had done something wrong, so he told them there was no room for them to stay with us. But grandma told them they could spend the night in our stable. Now it was beginning to make sense! My grandparents had told all of us one night that we could not go in the stable. Now I knew why.

Jesus was born that night! The angels told the shepherds about His birth. And Shimon, his dad, and the other shepherds came to see Jesus in the stable. The next morning, grandpa told Mary and Jesus they could stay in our house until they were ready to go home. But he said Joseph had to stay in Jerusalem.

. . .

"Sarah, you cannot tell anyone they are here," grandma said.

"Can I come help with the baby if I am very quiet about it?" I asked. Mary looked at my grandma and said it was okay with her. She would be happy for the company. Grandma said, "Then it's okay with me, as long as you don't let anyone see you."

For the next few weeks, I carefully made my way to the "empty" room each day to spend time with Mary and Jesus. Mary and I would talk as I held the baby. I would often stare into His eyes – and He would look right back into mine. I never wanted to leave the room when it was my time to go.

Nobody knew about my secret until last night! The sound of heavy footsteps walking upstairs woke us all up. I jumped out of bed to see what was going on. My sister and some of my cousins were already up.

. . .

We saw a group of men who looked important and were dressed very different from us. I knew they had come to see Jesus. A young boy carried a pretty box upstairs. It was a present for the baby! When the box was opened, a sweet smell filled the air. My parents and my aunts and uncles stood at the door looking inside.

We all watched as the strangers left our house. Then one by one, my family went into the room and met Jesus. Soon my grandpa walked into the room. I thought he might be angry at all of us for entering the room. But instead, he started crying and fell to his knees. It scared me a little because I had never seen my grandpa cry.

"I am so sorry, Mary," he said. "I am so very sorry I did not believe you and Joseph. I did not let you come into my home! I did not let the Son of God into my house! I turned my back on you – and Him! Mary, please forgive me!" Then he looked at baby Jesus and said, "God, please forgive me!"

. . .

I will never forget that special night – the night my family and I spent with Jesus. Joseph arrived the next morning to take Mary and Jesus to Jerusalem. But before they left, Joseph and Grandpa hugged for a very long time.

∼

About Sarah

Sarah and her family are not in the Bible. We do know that Bethlehem was Joseph's "ancestral" home. In those days, Bethlehem would have been a small, out-of-the-way place. Travelers would have stayed in homes – most likely with family. Joseph probably had family who lived in the town. And it is possible his family would have reacted much like Sarah's grandpa, when he said there was no room for them to stay. We know that Mary gave birth to Jesus in a stable. But we also know that about six weeks later, when the wise men visited Mary and Jesus, they were staying in a home in Bethlehem. This story explains how all of that might have happened.

You can read about the birth of Jesus in Luke 2:1-7 in the Bible.

∼

Ashriel with his great-grandfather in the Temple as
they see Jesus

ASHRIEL'S STORY

My name is Ashriel and I am ten years old. But in just a few weeks, my birthday will take place and I will be eleven! I live in the city of Jerusalem. Have you ever heard of Hanukkah? It is a special time when Jewish people like me celebrate our past.

A long time ago, a brave priest named Judas told our people not to obey our evil ruler. Our ruler did not want us to believe in God. He did evil things in the temple where we prayed. Our people revolted against him and defeated him. For the first time in many, many years, our people were not being told what to do by a ruler from another country.

Judas made our temple like new again. There were special lamps in the temple that used oil to make light. But not just any oil could be used. The oil had to be pure and it took eight days to make.

When the lamps were lit the first time, there was just enough oil for them to burn for only one day. But somehow these lamps stayed lit for eight days until the new oil was ready! My people believe God made this happen. So, every year we remember those eight days with a holiday called Hanukkah.

My great-grandfather Simeon is a priest. I call him Papa. He is one hundred thirteen years old! Every day he goes to the temple. God gave him a promise a long time ago – and he knows God always keeps His promises!

. . .

When he was sixteen years old, Papa was at the temple praying during Hanukkah. By that time, my people were again no longer free – the Roman emperor was telling us what to do. Papa prayed and asked God to help us be free again so we could pray and honor Him.

As Papa prayed, he heard a voice tell him, "Simeon, you will not die until you have seen My Son. Watch for Him and wait for Him!"

Every day since then, for many years, Papa has gone to the temple to watch for the Son of God. I now go to the temple with Papa to help him walk because he is so old and needs my help. Papa says that God chose for me to be born during Hanukkah for a special reason. God was reminding Papa that He would keep the promise He had made during Hanukkah a long time ago. That's why Papa asked my parents to name me Ashriel. My name means "God's promise."

. . .

Most every day he tells me, "Today could be the day we see Him!" Even though it has been almost one hundred years since God gave him that promise, Papa believes it as much today as he did when he was sixteen.

This morning, soon after we arrived at the temple, Papa saw a man and woman with an infant. The man was gently taking care of the young mother and the baby in her arms. We watched the man buy two birds called doves from a shop near the temple. He then gave the doves and some money to the priest as an offering.

Papa told me the baby must be a boy. He could tell from the offering the man gave that the baby was forty days old and was a firstborn son. Over the years, Papa had seen many parents with baby boys give a gift just like this one. And every time he thought it might be God's Son.

But this time was different. Papa seemed to be really happy. He told me to help him walk over to the baby. He said his heart was beating extra fast!

Papa asked the parents if he could see their child. They kindly turned their young Son so Papa could look into His eyes. Tears began to stream down my great-grandfather's cheeks.

He turned to the baby's mother and said, "This Child of yours will cause many people in Israel to fall and others to stand. The Child will be like a warning sign. Many people will reject Him, and you, young mother, will suffer as though you had been stabbed by a dagger. But all this will show what is really in the hearts of the people."[1]

She didn't say a word but simply nodded at Papa. She was so kind I could see why God chose her to be the mother of His Son. When Papa reached to pick up the baby, she willingly handed the tiny boy to him.

. . .

The baby didn't make a sound as Papa held Him. My great-grandfather looked up at heaven and said, *"Lord, I am Your servant, and now I can die in peace, because You have kept Your promise to me. With my own eyes I have seen what You have done to save Your people."*[2]

Papa gave the baby back to His mother and thanked God for her and the father. We stood there watching as the mother and father walked away with their child.

"These people have no idea what just happened," Papa said, as he pointed to the other people in the temple. "They don't know they have been in the same room with the Son of God. They came here to worship God and He has been right here with them, but they did not see Him. And sadly, when He appears before them again, more than likely they still will not recognize Him."

I quietly thanked God for keeping His promise to my great-grandfather. Then I thanked Him for keeping His promise to all of us. His promised Son had come, and He had allowed me to see Him, too. And I knew this wouldn't be the last time I would see Him.

~

About Ashriel

Ashriel is not in the Bible but Simeon is. [3] *Simeon was old, though we do not know his exact age. But he probably needed someone to help him walk around the temple. That person would likely have been a young family member. So, that person would have heard Simeon's prayer of praise over Jesus.*

You can read about Simeon in Luke 2:25-35 in the Bible.

~

Khati points Joseph to his father's shop on the
streets of Alexandria

KHATI'S STORY

Hi there! I'm Khati and I am eleven years old. I live in the city of Alexandria in Egypt. Our city is the largest city in the world and it is located right beside the Mediterranean Sea.

Every day I walk down to the water and watch ships arrive from all over the world. These ships carry supplies from faraway lands like China! A lot of times I hear people from these ships speaking words I don't understand. It is a fun place to live and grow up.

. . .

My father's name is Alim and he owns a business where he trades grain and something called papyrus for fancy cloth. Papyrus is used to make writing paper, but it is also used to make twisted rope. My dad trades a lot of rope and grain to the men on these ships in exchange for nice cloth from their countries. He also sells the cloth, paper, and grain to the people right here in our city. He is a very smart businessman.

He not only trades supplies at work, but he also trades for what we need as a family. My dad learned how to trade when he was a boy watching my grandfather. And I have been learning by watching my dad since I was young.

One of my daily chores is to trade for some of our food with buyers and sellers near the water. I love being right next to the sea to trade for fresh fish when the fishing boats come in with their daily catch. My favorite is sea bass, and my mom knows just how to cook it! But I also trade for chicken, beef, and all kinds of beans and peas. My mom uses the peas to make one of my favorite foods – falafel. You must try it sometime!

Two years ago, I was down near the water when I saw a man with his wife and baby. I could tell they were new in town. And I knew they were Jewish by the way they were dressed. They looked a little lost in our big city. The man was trying to trade for food for his family, but he wasn't having much success.

I went over and asked if I could help him. He was surprised that a young boy like me would offer to help. But I told him that my parents had taught me to help those in need whenever I could.

He said his name was Joseph and that he and his family had just come here from Jerusalem. They were planning to stay in Alexandria for a while. He needed to find food for his family and a place to stay. I told him not to worry, I was sure my father could help him!

· · ·

We went to my dad's business, and while Joseph and my dad talked, I went over to see the baby. His mother told me His name was Jesus. My younger brother was only a few months older than Jesus so I was used to being around babies. But there was something different about this baby. He seemed to know what was going on around Him. And when I looked into His eyes, He looked right back into mine. I could tell there was something special about Him.

Joseph told my dad he was a carpenter looking for work, and he needed a place for his family to stay. We owned a small house right next door to our home. My dad had been looking for someone to rent it.

Since my dad loved to trade, he told Joseph and his family they could live in our small house if Joseph would do some carpentry work for him. Joseph agreed, so he and his family moved in next door.

. . .

A few days later, my dad told me that Joseph was a better carpenter than anyone he had ever seen. He finished his work really fast. So my dad told some of his friends about Joseph's good work and soon a lot of people wanted him to do work for them. I was happy because that meant Joseph's family would keep living next door to us.

My mom and Mary soon became good friends. My mom, whose name is Nena, helped Mary get around in the big city. Since they both had young children, they had a lot in common.

Even though our families were very close, we did not talk about religion. Our family believed in the gods of the sun and the moon, and the earth and the sea. My dad said Joseph and Mary believed in one God. He told me Jewish people believed they were special in God's eyes.

It was about a year later that Mary told my mom a secret that changed our lives. She told my mom the story of how Jesus was born. She said an angel had told her she would give birth to the Son of God.

Then Mary told mom how the angel had spoken to her cousin and to Joseph. She said shepherds had heard the news from angels the night Jesus was born. And she told her about wise men who had followed a star to visit Jesus just a few weeks later.

Mary finished her story by saying an angel told Joseph to come to our town in Egypt to keep Jesus safe. All of this was a lot for anyone to believe!

But about a week later, we received news that a king had sent soldiers to kill all the little boys under two years old living in the place where Jesus had been born. Can you believe a king would do such a bad thing to kids? But my parents and I remembered what Mary had told my mom.

. . .

A few days later I was at my dad's business when I heard him talking to Joseph.

"Joseph," he said, "I know you are an honest man. And Mary told Nena how your God spoke to you and told you to come here – and how Jesus is His Son.

"But why would your God choose you and Mary to be the parents of His Son? Why wouldn't He choose a king and queen? Why would He allow His Son to be born in a stable instead of a palace? And why would He let a king try to kill Jesus?

"I don't understand any of this! Why would your God send angels to tell shepherds when Jesus was born instead of giving the news to important people? Why would He want His child to live in a tiny house in a poor area of Alexandria?"

. . .

Joseph smiled at me and my dad. "Because that is what He said He would do. He said His Son would be born of a virgin.[1] He said His Son would be born in Bethlehem.[2] He said He would be worshipped by shepherds, and foreign kings would bring gifts to Him.[3] He said a king would kill many children in an attempt to kill Him.[4] He said He would direct the Child to Egypt.[5] And He said so much more!

"He said His Son would grow up in a simple home.[6] And He said when He grows up Jesus will be punished for our sins.[7]

"Many years ago, God provided a ram in some bushes for our patriarch Abraham to offer as a sacrifice instead of his son Isaac. By faith Abraham had believed that God would provide the sacrifice. And he believed God would also one day provide His own perfect sacrifice to die for all of our sins.[8] I believe that one day Jesus will be that sacrifice – He will die for the sins of us all.[9] That is what I believe, and that is why I believe.

. . .

"Alim, I don't know why God chose me to be a father to His Son. I have never done anything to deserve it. And I don't know why He led us to you and your son on our first day here. Or why He chose you to help us, but I know that He did. You, Nena, and Khati are a part of God's plan. God does things in our lives so we will believe in Him and His Son.

"When I didn't know what to believe, I asked God to show me. Will you let Him show you, too?"

Joseph stood there silently for a few moments and then turned and walked away.

Later that night, I heard my dad tell my mom what Joseph said. When he finished, he said, "Nena, I believe." She smiled and said, "So do I." I walked into the room, looked at both of them, and said, "And, so do I!"

. . .

We were sad a few weeks later when Joseph said it was time for his family to go home to Nazareth. We would miss our friends, but we knew our lives had been changed forever. God brought Joseph's family here to protect Jesus, but He also brought them here so we could believe in Him!

~

About Khati

Khati is not in the Bible and neither is his family. We do not know what city in Egypt Joseph, Mary, and Jesus stayed in so King Herod wouldn't be able to kill Jesus. We only know they were in Egypt until the angel told Joseph through a dream that it was safe to return home.[10]

You can read about the journey of Joseph, Mary and Jesus to Egypt in Matthew 2:13-23 in the Bible.

~

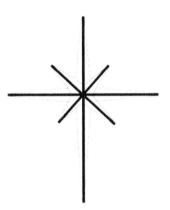

James receives a set of wooden animals and an ark
Jesus carved for him

JAMES'S (THE SON OF JOSEPH) STORY

I am a ten-year-old boy named James and I live in Nazareth. My parents are Joseph and Mary. I have a brother named Jesus who is almost three years older than I am.

After Jesus was born, my parents lived in Egypt for a couple of years, then they came back here to live. I was born soon after they returned. Our family has grown and now I have three younger brothers and two younger sisters.

Jesus has always been a good big brother. We sleep in the same room with our other brothers.

We play together. We explore together. As we've gotten older, we even work together. Jesus is helping our dad teach me how to be a carpenter and make my own set of tools.

When I was three years old, dad showed Jesus how to make toy wooden animals. He made some for me along with a small wooden ark, which is another name for a big boat. I would tell the story of Noah and the flood over and over as I played with the ark and the animals. When I was five, Jesus made dolls for me that looked like David and Goliath. I was so proud of those dolls! When friends came over to play, I used to tell them how our ancestor King David used a slingshot to kill the Philistine giant.

Jesus and I also played ball together with a ball we made out of an animal skin stuffed with husks. We enjoyed kicking the ball back and forth to each other. We also made up our own games with points for the longest or more difficult kicks.

. . .

Since Jesus is older, He has always been stronger than me. But that doesn't stop me from trying to beat Him! We try to see who can lift the heaviest stones over his head. Jesus always wins that game, but I found out I can run faster. We race each other or just go for a run together through the hills.

I wasn't very old when I learned that Jesus loves to read and study the Scripture. Early in the morning and at the end of each workday, Jesus often goes to the synagogue to read God's Word and ask questions of the rabbis there. Most of the time our brothers, Joseph and Jude, and I go with Him.

I wish I was more like Jesus. He never says bad words or is mean to anyone – including our parents, teachers, neighbors, or other kids. No matter how hard I try to be like Him, I always do something I'm not supposed to do. Or sometimes I don't do my chores. I really get in trouble for that! But Jesus always remembers to do His, and He never complains about it.

· · ·

A few months ago, our entire family went to Jerusalem to celebrate Passover. Remember, Passover is the festival for Jewish people to thank God for freeing our people from slavery. The day after we got there, our family went to the temple to pray and honor God.

After a while, Jesus walked over to where the rabbis were teaching. I decided to go sit with Him. Jesus started asking questions, giving answers, and saying verses from Scripture. I could never talk in front of other people like He does! I don't think some of the men there liked it, either, because He was so young. But Jesus is really smart, and He knows so much about Scripture that the men didn't say anything.

Every day we were in Jerusalem, Jesus went to the temple to talk with the rabbis. I joined Him a couple of times, and each time more and more people came to see the young boy who seemed to know more about the Scriptures than the rabbis did.

. . .

The next day, we were headed home when my mother asked if I knew where Jesus was. Jesus had walked with the older boys on our way to Jerusalem, so my parents thought He was with them that day, too. I'll be glad when I'm old enough to walk with the older boys instead of having to stay by my mother's side!

But none of the boys had seen Him. This wasn't like Jesus. He never did anything wrong! My parents were worried so they went back to Jerusalem to find Him. My uncle Clopas went with them. The rest of my brothers and sisters and I headed home with my aunt Mary. My dad told me to help my aunt take care of my brothers and sisters. This was the first time he had given me the job of being a big brother – and I was very proud!

My parents and uncle got home with Jesus a few days later. My parents said they found Jesus with the teachers in the temple. I wasn't surprised since He went there every chance He got.

.   .   .

But two days later, my parents told me something about Jesus I could hardly believe. They said Jesus and I have the same mother but different fathers. My parents told me that Jesus's father is God! They told me that the Spirit of God had come upon my mom while she was still a virgin and she became pregnant with Jesus. They told me the story of how the angel had come to them, and how they had gone to Bethlehem. They told me how the angels had announced His birth to a group of shepherds, and how wise men from the east had brought Him gifts.

That's why Jesus had gone to the temple so much! It is His Father's house! For almost ten years, I had looked up to Jesus as my big brother. Now I found out my brother is the Son of God.

Some things make more sense now – like how He knows so much about Scripture and why He never does anything wrong. But I also know things will never be the same between us.

. . .

Is He my brother or my God? He can't be both ... or can He? I hope someday I will find the answers to all my questions.

~

About James, the son of Joseph

James is the son of Joseph and Mary. He is the half brother of Jesus. Growing up, James was a younger brother of Jesus. Jesus, James, and the other three sons of Joseph, together with at least two daughters, would have been like any other family. They would have played together, worked together, laughed together, and sometimes even cried together. James, and the rest of Jesus' half brothers, did not believe Jesus was the Son of God until after Jesus arose from the dead.[1] After that, James became a follower of Jesus and became a leader of the early church.

James and the other half brothers and sisters of Jesus are mentioned in Mark 6:1-6 in the Bible.

~

John the Baptizer as a teenager in Qumran

JOHN'S STORY

Hi! My name is John and I am twelve years old. I grew up in Hebron and my parents were Zechariah and Elizabeth. I am my parents' only child and they were both very old when I was born. They both died a year ago and I came to live with my cousin Adriel and his wife, Joanna. They live with a group of people called the Essenes in this place called Qumran.

My parents often told me the story of how I came to be born. My father was a priest in the temple in Jerusalem. Remember, a temple is the place we go to pray and bring offerings to God. One day an angel came to my dad and said,

"Don't be afraid, Zechariah! God has heard your prayer. Your wife, Elizabeth, will give you a son, and you are to name him John. He will be filled with the Holy Spirit, even before his birth. He will prepare the people for the coming of the Lord."[1]

The angel's appearance made my dad afraid. Because of his fear, he didn't believe what the angel was telling him! How could my mom have a baby at her age? And how could I be the messenger to tell the people that the Son of God was coming? But instead of asking questions so he could understand, my dad chose not to believe the angel. And because my dad didn't believe the angel, God would not let him talk again until after I was born.

When my father got home from the temple, he wanted to tell my mother what the angel had said. But since he couldn't talk, he motioned with his hands and wrote words in the sand and on a tablet. Eventually my mom understood, and soon after she became pregnant with me.

. . .

About six months later, my mom's younger cousin, Mary, came to visit her. My mother told me that I jumped inside her belly when I heard Mary's voice. Somehow, even while I was in my mom's belly I knew that the baby in Mary's belly was the One I would tell the world about.

Mary stayed with my mother for three months then went back home to Nazareth just before I was born. When Mary got home she married a carpenter named Joseph. I remember seeing Mary and Joseph with their son when I was four and again when I was six. Both times, we were all in Jerusalem to celebrate Passover. I don't remember much about them except their son, Jesus, and I were both young boys.

When I was seven, my father became very sick. He was no longer able to travel. We remained in my hometown of Hebron and never again re-turned to Jerusalem to celebrate Passover. So I didn't see Jesus after that.

. . .

My father taught me from the Bible from the time I was very little. He taught me about the promises of God, including those about His Son. He taught me to honor God in how I live and what I say.

After my parents died, I came to live with my cousin and his family here in Qumran. They live a very simple life and they eat a lot of different foods, like locusts and wild honey. I didn't even know what a locust was – do you? It's a bug, kind of like a grasshopper. Believe it or not, I even learned to like them!

My cousins' clothes are not what I'm used to wearing, either. Joanna made a shirt for me from camel hair. It's kind of itchy – a lot different from the soft shirts my mom used to make me. But I have gotten used to wearing it.

God is using my time here with my cousin to show me how I will prepare people for the coming of the Son of God. The Essenes do something as a part of their worship of God they call baptism. The people step into a river or a pool of water just like you and I step into a bath to clean the dirt off of our bodies. Then, when we come out of the bath we are clean.

But baptism is different. When we step into the water to be baptized it means that we have asked God to clean our hearts. We have asked Jesus to forgive us of our sins. And now we have chosen to follow Jesus for the rest of our lives knowing that He is the Son of God. Baptism doesn't clean my heart like the bath cleans my body. Instead, baptism tells others that Jesus has already cleaned my heart and I am following Him.

That's what the angel meant when he said I was to prepare the people for the coming of Jesus. I will tell the people to turn from their sin and turn to Him. And I will baptize those who have chosen to turn to Him. Who knows, maybe they will call me John the Baptizer!

.   .   .

God used my parents, and now is using Adriel and Joanna, to get me ready for the work He wants me to do. I know that one day I will see His Son, Jesus, again. I know my heart will jump in my chest, just like I jumped in my mother's belly the first time we met. Until then, I will tell everyone I meet about Him and that He is coming to save us from our sins.

How about you? You're not too little to know. What will you tell others about Jesus?

~

About John

The Bible tells us about the birth of John the Baptist as well as his ministry as an adult, but we do not know anything about his years in between. We do not know the date his parents died. It may have been after he was grown. But because of their old age at his birth, it is possible they died while he was still young. If that is the case, he would have been raised by a trusted family member.

You can read about the birth of John the baptizer in Luke 1:57-80 in the Bible.

PLEASE HELP ME BY LEAVING A REVIEW!

~

i would be very grateful if you would leave a review of this book. Your feedback will be helpful to me in my future writing endeavors and will also assist others as they consider picking up a copy of the book.

To leave a review, go to:

amazon.com/dp/B088SLCMXX

Thanks for your help!

~

THE STORY CONTINUES ...

For the entire family

Little Did We Know

THE EYEWITNESSES COLLECTION BOOK #1

This book is a collection of twenty-five short stories for the advent season from some familiar and some not-so-familiar people. These stories have been written with teens and adults in mind. Experience the truth of the glorious arrival of the baby in the manger through the lens of these fictional, first-person accounts of the prophecies and events heralding the birth of Jesus.

Little Did They Know and *Not Too Little To Know* are companion books. Each of the ten children in *Not Too Little To Know* also make an appearance in *Little Did They Know*. Both books stand alone, but they can also be used in conjunction with one another to help further family conversations about the advent.

Exclusively available through Amazon.

Though the Eyes of a Shepherd

Read the continuing story of Shimon, the shepherd boy in the stable, as he re-encounters Jesus at the Jordan, then follows Him through the wilderness to the cross and the empty tomb. This novel has been written with teens and adults in mind. See the Savior through a shepherd's eyes and experience a story of redemption – the redemption of a shepherd – and the redemption of each one who chooses to follow the Good Shepherd. Available now through your online bookstore.

For information on all of my books, go to wildernesslessons.com or kenwinter.org

WildernessLessons

ALSO AVAILABLE AS AN AUDIOBOOK

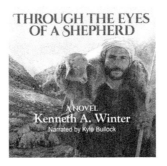

SCRIPTURE BIBLIOGRAPHY

~

Much of the story line of this book is taken from the Bible – specifically from the Gospels according to Matthew and Luke. The first story about Abraham and Isaac is taken from the Book of Genesis. Certain fictional events or depictions of those events have been added.

Some of the dialogue in the book is a direct quote from the Bible. Those places are *italicized* in the book and have a number after them. If you want to see where those statements are in the Bible, the reference is listed below.

Also, you will find numbers where the words are not italicized. Those references are to help you better understand some of the statements that have been made in the book. The Bible is the best place to read more about them!

From the author

(1) John 3:16

(2) Luke 19:10

(3) 1 John 1:9

Chapter 1

(1) Genesis 12:2-3 (TLB)

(2) Genesis 16:2 (CEV)

(3) Genesis 17:21 (paraphrase)

(4) Genesis 22:2 (CEV)

(5) Genesis 22:7 (TLB)

(6) Genesis 22:8 (GNT)

(7) Genesis 22:11-12 (GNT)

(8) Genesis 22:16-18 (CEV)

Chapter 2

[1] Luke 1:30-31 (ICB)

[2] Luke 1:34

[3] Luke 1:35 (ICB)

Chapter 3

[1] John 19:25; Luke 24:18

[2] Matthew 10:3

[3] Mark 14:40

[4] Mark 3:18

Chapter 4

[1] Luke 2:10-11

[2] Luke 2:14 (GNT)

[3] Luke 2:15

Chapter 7

[1] Luke 2:34-35 (CEV-paraphrase)

[2] Luke 2:29-30 (CEV)

(3) Luke 2:25-35

Chapter 8

(1) Isaiah 7:14

(2) Micah 5:2

(3) Psalm 72:9-10

(4) Jeremiah 31:15

(5) Hosea 11:1

(6) Isaiah 53:2

(7) Isaiah 53:3-6

(8) Genesis 22:8-14

(9) Isaiah 53:6

(10) Luke 2:13-23

Chapter 9

(1) Luke 1:13, 15, 17

Chapter 10

(1) 1 Corinthians 15:7; Acts 1:14

ACKNOWLEDGMENTS

I do not cease to give thanks for you ....
Ephesians 1:16 (ESV)

~

to my wife, life partner, collaborator and best
friend, LaVonne,
for faithfully trusting God throughout every
step of our faith adventure together, and for
your beautiful narration of the audiobook;

to my family,
for your support and encouragement;

to Carley,

for the giftedness God has given you, and the
way you allowed Him to use you to bring the
characters to life;

to Sheryl,
for helping me craft the stories of the advent of
Jesus for a younger audience;

to Dennis,
for always using your talent to bring glory
to God;

and most importantly,
to the One without whom there would be no
story
– **our Lord and Savior Jesus Christ** –
who invites children of all ages to come to Him.

~

ABOUT THE AUTHOR

 **Ken Winter** is a follower of Jesus, an extremely blessed husband, and a proud father and grandfather – all by the grace of God. His journey with Jesus has led him to serve on the pastoral staffs of two local churches – in West Palm Beach, Florida and Richmond, Virginia – and as the vice president of mobilization of the International Mission Board of the Southern Baptist Convention.

Carley Elder is the talented artist who created all of the beautiful illustrations in this book. This is her debut work, and we look forward to seeing

much more from her in the days ahead.

To read Ken's weekly blog posts and see information about the other books he has written, go
to kenwinter.org.

Printed in Great Britain
by Amazon

12077026R00068